I CAN SLEEP WHEN THE WIND BLOWS

Retold by Heather L. Davis

Illustrated by Roberta Malasomma

This book is dedicated to my beloved grandfather, Harold Rogers, who set an example for me as a very hard worker and he told me this story when I was a little girl.

This is also dedicated to my husband Roman and my amazing children Justun, Dagan, Trinity, Lleyton, Chloe, Kaylyn, Morgan, and Skye who make my life complete. I love you all so much! Thank you for being so supportive and wonderful!

Library of Congress Control Number: 2016917604

ISBN-13: 978-1539502166
ISBN-10: 1539502163

Print information available on the last page

Rev. date: 10/06/2016

CreateSpace Independent Publishing Platform,
North Charleston, SC

Long ago, on a lonely, windy plain, there lived a farmer who owned a large farm.

The farmer needed someone to help him take care of all the animals on his farm, so he put out an ad for farmhands.

The farmer expected a lot of people to apply, but on the day he planned to hold the interviews, only one boy came.

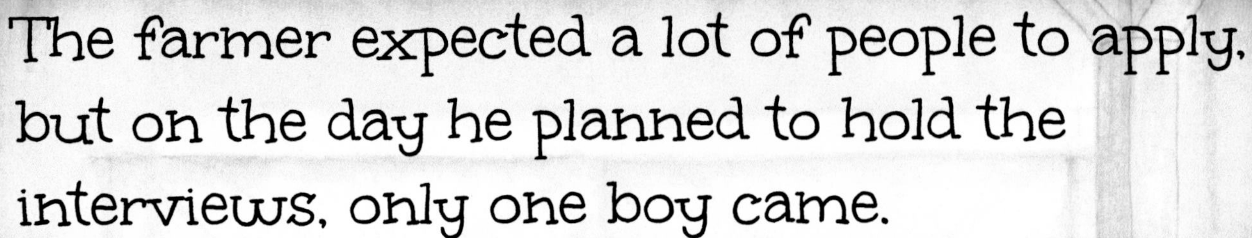

The boy's name was Jim. Jim was 17 years old, tall and thin with blonde hair and big blue eyes.

As the farmer looked at Jim, he wasn't sure he would be strong enough to do the hard work that had to be done on his farm.

He asked the boy why he should hire him to work on his farm.

Jim looked at the farmer and simply said, "I can sleep when the wind blows."

The farmer was confused and asked Jim what he meant. Jim looked at him and said again, "I can sleep when the wind blows."

The farmer didn't understand what the boy meant, but he needed help with his farm, so he hired Jim.

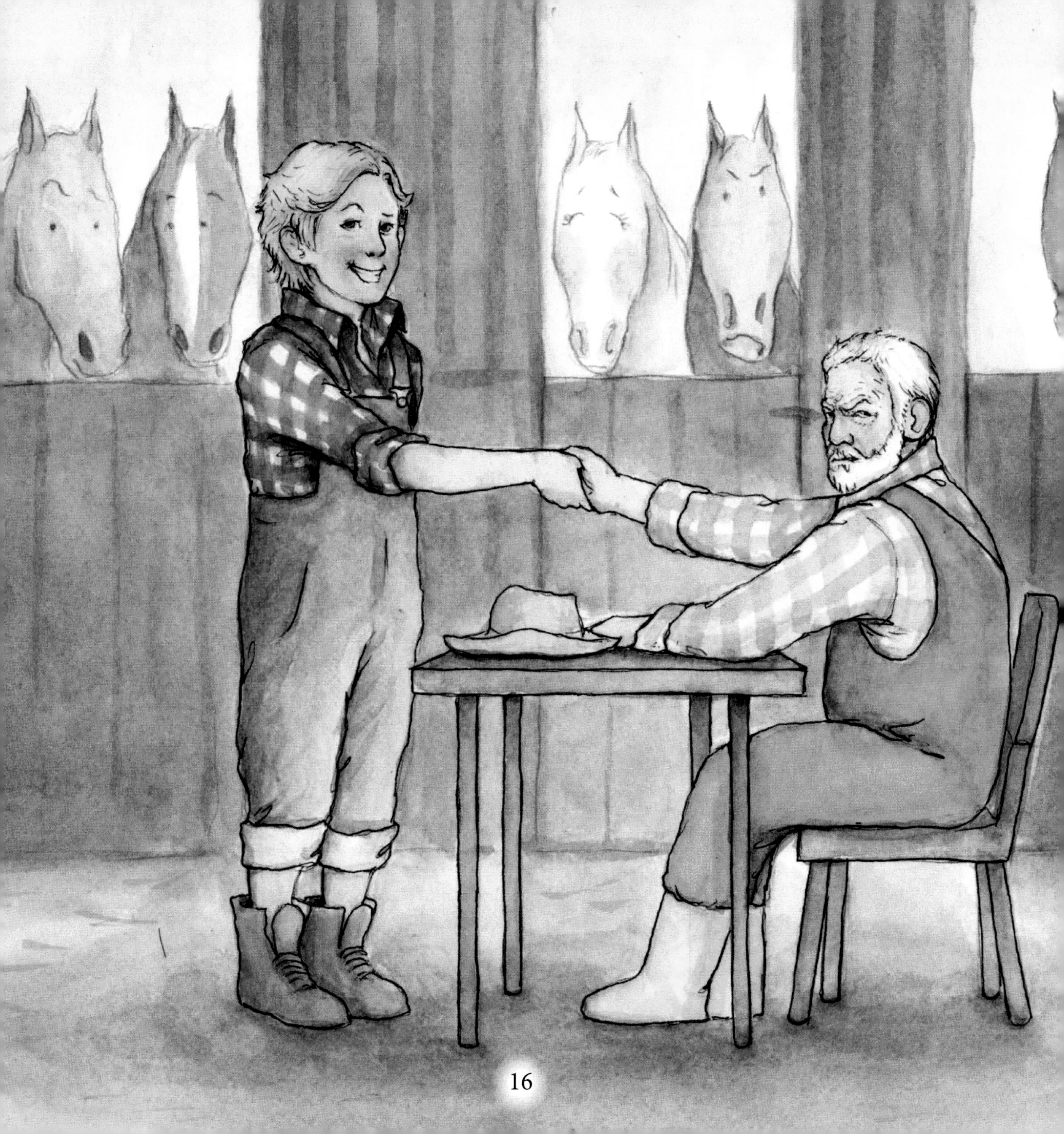

Jim was a good worker. He worked hard and did his job well. He was the first one awake each morning, and he was the last one working each night. The farmer was happy he hired him.

One night, there was a terrible storm. The wind roared, and the rain pounded the ground.

In a panic, the farmer ran to wake up Jim.

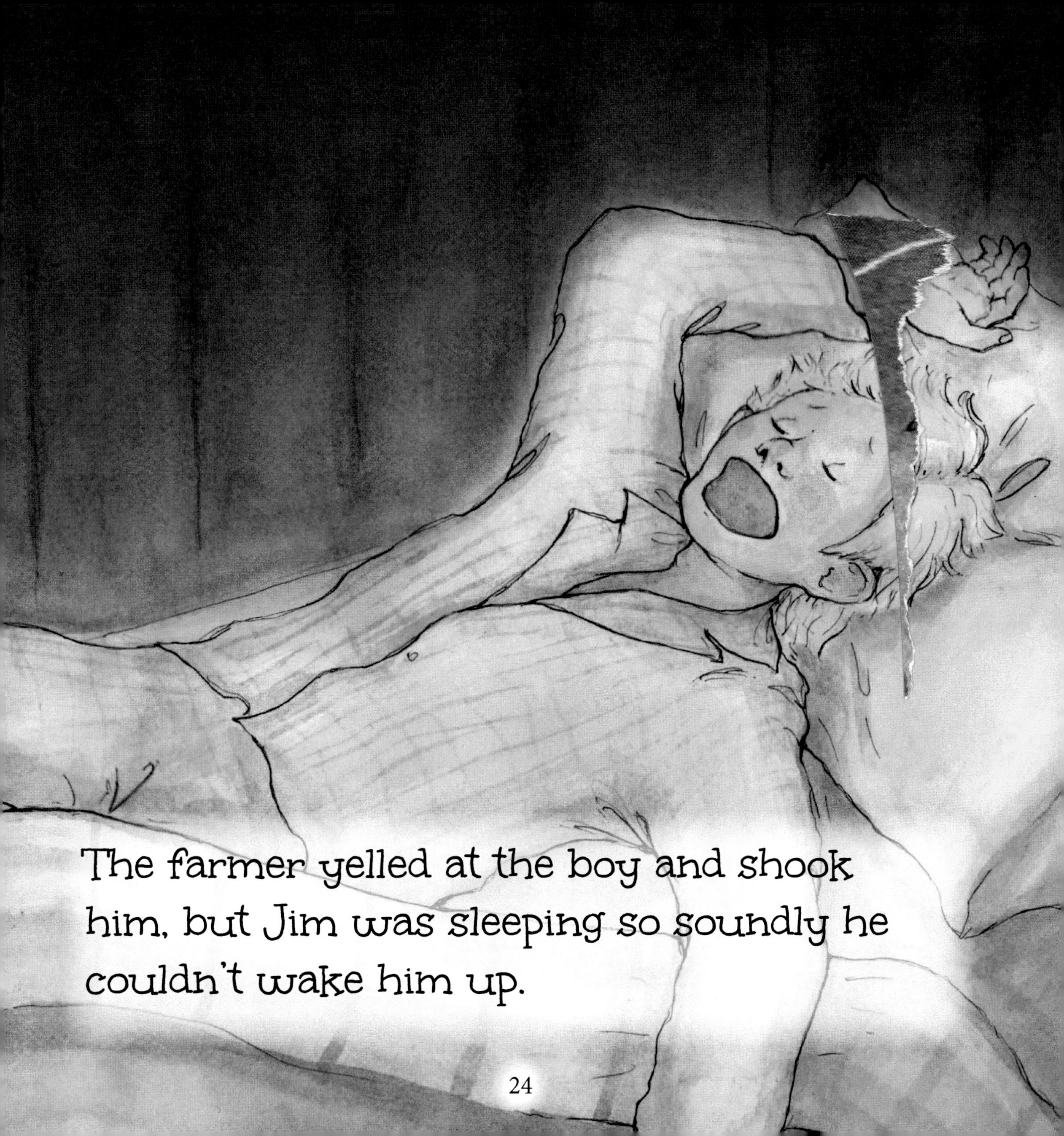

The farmer yelled at the boy and shook him, but Jim was sleeping so soundly he couldn't wake him up.

Finally, angry and tired, the farmer went out alone to do the hard work of getting his farm ready for a storm.

The farmer went to gather the animals and put them in the barn, but when he got there, he found all the animals safely tucked in and the barn securely latched.

The farmer went to tie down the hay, but he found the hay was already tightly tied down. As the farmer went to each of the areas in his farm, he found everything prepared to withstand the storm.

Confused and wet, the farmer went back to his house and went to sleep.

In the morning, the farmer asked Jim how he knew there was going to be a storm and when he prepared the farm.

The boy smiled and told the farmer he didn't know there was a storm coming. "I told you," Jim said, "I can sleep when the wind blows."

"I do those things every night so I can always sleep soundly knowing I'll be safe and prepared for any storm that may come."

Made in the USA
Middletown, DE
14 November 2020